B IN THE WORLD

B IN THE WORLD

SHARON MENTYKA

ILLUSTRATIONS BY STEPHEN SCHLOTT

Text copyright © 2014 by Sharon Mentyka
Illustrations copyright © 2014 by Stephen Schlott

Mentyka, Sharon.
Seven-year-old B Browning sometimes feels like wearing overalls and a flannel shirt and
other days wakes up wishing he could dress like his sister Patti-Anne and faces many
challenges and bullying because he's different.
ISBN 978-0-9863293-0-2 (trade)
ISBN 978-0-9863293-1-9 (e-book)

Printed in the United States of America
December 2014
First Edition

The text of this book is set in Egyptian Slate Standard and the display type is Amatic.
Book design by Stephen Schlott.

For more information: www.sharonmentyka.com

For Henry, who inspired this story.

And for the real "Mr. J."

Contents

Chapter 1:
The House on Lemon Street

B's given name was Blaine Powell Browning but no one
ever called him that. This was because when B was born,
his parents took a very long time choosing a name. So long
in fact, that everyone just began calling him "B" for baby.
By the time they finally decided on Blaine, a combination of
their names, Bob and Elaine, it was too late. B had already
stuck.

So Blaine Powell Browning became just "B."

B liked being just B. Blaine Powell was much too big a
name for a seven-year old anyway. He also liked sharing a
letter with a character in one of his favorite books. And just
like Junie B. Jones, B loved lemon pie and had a full head of
fiery red hair that he wore long and curly.

B especially liked hearing the story of how he'd come to be "just B" almost as much as his mother loved to tell it. This happened on a regular basis—at the dentist, at the playground, in the grocery store, pretty much whenever B met someone new.

"And what's your name?" people would ask.

B would answer, then wait. The person, almost always an adult, would tilt their head a little to the left or right, as if they'd suddenly gotten a bit of a kink in their neck or felt a headache coming on. Then they would ask how he wound up with such an unusual name. And that would be the signal for B's mother to launch into her story.

If B's older sister Patti-Anne were there, she would sigh and frown, trying to get their mother to hurry up with her storytelling. Sometimes Patti-Anne would tap her foot, pull on their mother's arm, or simply begin walking away so that B's mother had no choice but to finish up and hurry along after.

Whenever that happened, B felt very sorry for Patti-Anne. Even though she was four years older, how boring it must be to have such an ordinary name that nobody ever asked about. B knew it made Patti-Anne sad too, because once when he was helping his mother fold the laundry, he'd asked how his parents had picked his sister's name. B's mother stopped mid-fold and a dreamy look had come over her face. Patti-Anne had perked up, eager to finally hear her story. But then his mother just shrugged.

"Your father and I just liked the name," she said, smoothing flat B's favorite flannel pajamas.

Whenever B remembered that, he felt very lucky.

• • •

B and Patti-Anne lived with their mother and father in a comfy, old house on Lemon Street. B liked nearly everything about the house. He liked that there were enough sidewalks and roads nearby that he could roller-skate and run races, but not too many sidewalks and roads that birds wouldn't nest in the trees. Roller-skating, running races, and watching birds and butterflies were some of the things B liked to do best.

B liked that his street was named "Lemon" and not "3rd" or "4th" Street. Whoever named it had made a good decision because lots and lots of lemon trees grew there. It made living on Lemon Street feel very special. If he had lived on 3rd or 4th Street, what would he have found there? Threes and fours?

B liked the lemon trees that grew on Lemon Street. Sometimes, when his bedroom windows were open, the air smelled sweet and almost sugary. Anytime he wanted, he could simply go outside and pluck a lemon from any one of those lemon trees and squeeze the juice out to make lemonade. Whenever B picked a lemon, he was always sure to wear something yellow. Wearing yellow just seemed to make sense, and yellow was one of his favorite colors anyway. Pink was his other favorite color, but wearing pink was tricky and it sometimes caused trouble. Lemony-yellow was safer.

Living on Lemon Street, B knew *everything* there was to know about lemons.

He knew that lemons should be a little bit green when you picked them.

He knew that an ordinary lemon contained about three tablespoons of juice, and that to get the most juice, you should roll the lemon on a counter to burst its tiny juice-filled cells.

He even knew that the white part of the peel just under the top yellow layer, called the zest, was very, very bitter and should never be used in cooking. This was an important thing to know because B also liked to cook, especially with lemons.

Last month, for Patti-Anne's birthday, B had wanted to make a special lemon cake four layers high with lemony butter icing. He imagined pouring icy glasses of lemonade and serving them up with a thin slice of lemon perched perfectly on the rim of each glass. B thought it would all be very fancy and might even distract Patti-Anne from the

Wearing Pink Was Tricky

memory of the ordinary name she had been given on her birthday eleven years ago.

But when he told his sister his special idea, her eyes had narrowed.

"Just stay out of the way," she'd growled. "I don't want my friends to see you prancing around in Mom's apron cooking, like some kind of top chef."

Patti-Anne hadn't always been so mean. But after graduating from fifth grade last June, she had announced to the whole family how "incredibly relieved" she was to be "getting on with my life." It seemed to B that the only thing Patti-Anne was getting was meaner and bossier. All she

JUST STAY OUT OF THE WAY!

seemed to care about now was what her friends did, said, and thought, mostly about each other and especially about her.

B missed the old Patti-Anne who used to let him spend time in her room, flipping through movie magazines. Together they would *ooh* and *ahh* at the fabulous outfits the movie stars and models were wearing in the pictures. Sometimes Patti-Anne would let B hunt around in her closet and put together his own fashion show.

B wasn't really sure why one day he felt like wearing overalls and a flannel shirt, and the next day he'd wake up wishing he could dress like Patti-Anne. But he did know that the way he looked and the things he liked to do sometimes bothered and confused people.

Even Patti-Anne.

Lately, B could hardly step across the threshold to Patti-Anne's room without setting off her bossy alarm. And the last time he asked if he could borrow one of her scarves, she had exploded.

"You know Mom doesn't like it when you do that," she said, whirling around to face him and frightening him with her scowl.

B had slumped down on the floor in the hallway and stayed there for a long time. What Patti-Anne said wasn't even exactly true. His mother really didn't mind if he wore his sister's clothes in the house. She just wasn't okay with him wearing them outside...or to school.

Besides—it just felt right to B, so what was he supposed to do?

After that, for the whole summer, while Patti-Anne was getting on with her life, B had stayed out of her way. But starting tomorrow, he wouldn't have to worry about his sister so much anymore. Tomorrow, he would officially be a second grader in Mr. J's class, and everything would change. He was all ready. He'd even made a big batch of lemony cupcakes to bring along. Second grade was going to be awesome, he was sure of it.

After all, Mr. J had a one-letter name.

Just like B.

Chapter 2:
Rules of Room 2A

Early the next morning, B waited at the bus stop with Patti-Anne. He was wearing his favorite orange sweatpants, a yellow and orange t-shirt he'd been given after running a track meet last summer and his pink, white and orange checkered sneakers. His day-glo yellow backpack was freshly stocked with a new pencil case, two notebooks and Bugsy, his stuffed rabbit, who he liked having with him when he went to new places.

B stood very still, waiting for the bus, carefully holding his box of iced lemon cupcakes. But inside he was wild with impatience.

He was impatient for the bus to arrive.

He was impatient to see his friends Grace and Rudy who had been away the last few weeks of the summer at the beach, in the mountains, and visiting family.

He was impatient because he was no longer a first grader, but wouldn't officially be a second grader in Mr. J's class until he stepped inside his new classroom. And for that to happen the bus needed to come and take him to school *now.*

B couldn't wait to meet Mr. J. Everyone at New Horizons School said he was a very kind and fair teacher. Best of all, Mr. J filled his classroom with everything Mickey Mouse and at the end of the year the whole class had a sleepover at school. B had made a special cupcake for his new teacher with a big "J" written on it with bright blue icing.

"It's going to be a lot different than first grade, you know." Patti-Anne, who had been in Mr. J's class years and years and years ago, interrupted B's thinking. "Second grade has a lot more rules."

His sister looked him up and down, studying his sweatpants, t-shirt and sneakers. Then she scrunched her face up in a scowl. "First impressions mean *everything.*"

But this morning, B did not care what his sister said. He knew rules were important and were there to keep people safe, but sometimes they didn't always make sense to him. He wasn't going to let worrying about rules ruin his first day with Mr. J.

Still, B felt a little shiver run down his back as the big

yellow school bus rolled up to the curb and the black door wheezed open. Patti-Anne bounded up the steps. B took a deep breath and followed.

By the time the bus arrived at New Horizons School, B had forgotten all about his sister's warnings. Without a good-bye, Patti-Anne raced off to chatter with her friends. The new little kindergartners huddled behind their parents' legs and made him feel very grown up.

B spotted Rudy and Grace, and hurried over.

"Look what I brought for the whole class—and for Mr. J!" B said, lifting the lid on his box of cupcakes.

Rudy and Grace exchanged worried looks.

"Haven't you heard?" Rudy asked.

B shook his head. Rudy was the smartest kid in B's

class. He always knew the latest news about everything. Once, he'd shown B how you could put together important bits of news by paying particular attention to passing conversations between teachers and parents in the hallways.

"Rudy found out Mr. J isn't coming back," Grace said. She looked very sad. "We're going to have a new teacher."

What!? B couldn't believe what his friends were saying. He'd been waiting to be in Mr. J's class *forever*. The box of cupcakes suddenly felt so heavy he was afraid he might drop them. But there was no time to think because just then the bell rang across the schoolyard and all the students scuffled and tumbled into the building.

"Uh-oh," Rudy said when they were halfway down the hall. "Look."

At the door to what used to be Mr. J's classroom, the little Mickey Mouse figures that had always paraded merrily around the frame were gone. Now Room 2A's door looked like any other in the school—plain and bare.

They stepped inside.

"Oh, no!" Grace gasped. "It's all gone!"

The giant cutout of Mickey in his rainbow suit that had always greeted new second graders at New Horizons School had been taken down. B could see the faintest outline of where it had been taped to the wall.

Along the bookshelf under the wide windows, the Mickey Mouse pens, pencils and pencil sharpeners had vanished. The brightly colored Mickey boxes that held crayons, erasers, rubber bands and bottles of glue had all been replaced with plain brown cardboard ones labeled with thick black marker. And the Mickey ears that, according to Patti-Anne were supposed to be perched on the globe, were missing, too.

But worst of all, there was no Mr. J in Room 2A.

Instead, in his place stood a scary-looking woman wearing a navy-blue suit and sneakers and carrying a clipboard. Her grey-brown hair was pulled back tightly from her face. She had a pointy chin and one long eyebrow. She didn't look very happy to be in Room 2A at all.

"Hurry in now, children, hurry in," the woman called out. Her voice sounded to B like crinkling aluminum foil. "Take your seats. Quickly now. I've taped each of your names to your assigned desk."

All the children scurried up and down the aisles looking for their seats.

"I am Ms. Hitchings," the woman announced to the class, putting on a pair of heavy grey glasses. She silently surveyed the class, frowning.

"Where's Mr. J?" Grace raised her hand and called out bravely.

The whole class watched as Ms. Hitchings' single eyebrow slowly lifted but she answered anyway.

"Mr. Jones has unexpectedly taken ill, so I shall be your teacher this year. We'll get along quite well as long as everyone follows my rules. The first and most important one, I will tell you right now."

B was only half-listening. Dazed, he wandered Room 2A, still looking for his seat.

"Rule #1—No sugar of any kind shall be brought into my room. It serves no nutritional purpose and consuming it only makes children hyperactive. That includes all candies, cookies, ice cream, soda, juice or any sugared beverages."

B suddenly felt Ms. Hitchings close beside him.

"Do you need some help finding your seat, young lady?" she rasped.

B turned to face his new teacher, very glad that his box of cupcakes was between them.

"I'm—I'm B," he mumbled. "And I'm a boy."

Ms. Hitchings adjusted her glasses and looked B up and down as if he was a bug. "Oh yes, I see that now. Well, isn't your outfit quite...colorful?" She coughed. "Do you have a real name so we can get you seated?"

"B is my real name," he announced, proudly. "B. Browning."

"Browning...Browning..." She checked her clipboard.

"Oh yes. Here you are. Blaine Powell Browning."

"It's B," he repeated, in a softer voice this time.

"B is not a name. It is a letter," Ms. Hitchings declared. "In *my* class, students report by their given names. Besides, I already have you listed as Blaine Powell, so we'll just keep it that way, shall we?" She half-smiled, half-scowled at B. "Third row, second seat."

Her thin fingers quivered as she pointed the way and B thought for sure he saw a few long hairs poking out from the top of her hand.

"And what would be in your box, Blaine Powell?" Ms. Hitching looked down her nose at him.

B stared at the pure white box he still held tightly in his hands.

"They're cupcakes. Lemon ones. I made them for the class, and—,"

"I'll take that, thank you," Ms. Hitchings interrupted and before B could say another word, she lifted the box out of his hands and whisked it to the front of the room, tucking it away under her desk near the trashcan.

A few soft snickers rippled through the classroom. Surprised, B stumbled to his seat, feeling the heat rising in his face and hands. Taped to the top of his desk was a large white rectangle of paper with "Blaine Powell" written out in plain block letters in ordinary black marker. No Mickey

Mouse stickers. No happy faces. Nothing.

"Don't feel bad," Rudy whispered from across the next row. "Look." He pointed to his white rectangle where B could see the name "Rudolph" written in black letters.

Grateful, B returned Rudy's smile but it didn't really make him feel much better. At the front of the room, Ms. Hitchings droned on.

"Rule #2— I expect each and every one of you to...."

Patti-Anne was right after all. Second grade did have a lot of rules. And it was nothing like B had imagined.

CHAPTER 3:
FIVE FUN FACTS

The first week of second grade went just as badly as the first day. Ms Hitchings had so many rules it was almost easier to remember what you *could* do rather than what you couldn't.

"I told you so," Patti-Anne laughed when B told her about the horrors of second grade, which was really no help at all.

In the morning, before the bell, girls needed to line up on the right side of the playground, boys needed to line up on the left.

You couldn't eat your snack on the circle time rug.

You couldn't eat your snack in your seat.

You couldn't eat your snack after snack time.

"Maybe it's better if we just don't eat at all," Rudy groaned, after Ms. Hitchings handed out a long list of 'unacceptable snack foods.'

But it didn't take long for B to decide which of Ms. Hitchings' rules he hated most of all.

Room 2A didn't have its own bathroom like kindergarten and first grade. Since second graders were big kids now, they needed to use the big kid bathrooms outside in the hall or the extra big private bathroom downstairs near the art room. That bathroom was for anyone who needed extra help or used a wheelchair but B liked it better than the big, noisy, excitable boys' restroom.

Ms. Hitching was just finishing a lesson on the feeding habits of the scarlet rattler when B raised his hand.

"I need to use the bathroom, please, Ms. Hitchings," he asked in his most polite voice.

"Very well," Ms. Hitchings nodded. "Directly across the hall, please."

B stopped a few feet from the door.

"But—I'd rather use the big, quiet one."

Ms. Hitchings turned and looked at B as if he'd asked to use the bathroom on Mars.

"I think the boys restroom across the hall will be just fine," she said icily.

"But—my mom says I can always ask to use the—"

"Blaine Powell, I think we can follow the rules of my classroom, can't we?"

B sighed. He knew that was one of those questions adults asked that didn't really need answering. As he closed the classroom door behind him, B heard the sound of muffled laughter again, and this made him wonder. Since Ms. Hitchings had arrived, something peculiar had happened to the students in Room 2A.

Last year, almost all his classmates were nice to each other. It was the way their teacher, Mrs. Connor had taught them to be. If someone said something mean, or tried to grab someone else's toy, Mrs. Connor would sit them down for a time out and ask them to be more cooperative. Usually it worked.

But ever since Ms. Hitchings had arrived, with her grey-brown hair and one long eyebrow, frowning and criticizing, some of the kids seemed to be following her example. Now, they would laugh if one of their classmates made a mistake, or snicker when they got hurt.

"They think it'll keep the ax from falling on them," Rudy said when B asked if he'd noticed the change, too.

B thought he was probably right, but Grace was outraged. After just four days, she was fed up with Ms. Hitchings and her morphing classmates and was planning all sorts of ways to protest. As for B, he was just getting sadder and sadder.

On Thursday afternoon, Ms. Hitchings asked everyone to prepare five fun facts about themselves to present to the class the next day.

"It will be a way for me to get to know you," she said with a stiff smile.

Normally, B would have looked forward to an activity like "Five Fun Facts Day." He might even have baked some cupcakes to show that he liked to cook. But coming to school wasn't as much fun as it used to be. All he wanted was for this terrible first week to be over. Besides, he had a sneaky suspicion that sharing his favorite things with Ms. Hitchings wouldn't go over very well.

But "Five Fun Facts Day" had to proceed. On Friday, one by one, the kids in Room 2A presented their fun facts. Olivia talked about how she loved cats, macaroni and cheese, One Direction, ballet, and gymnastics.

"Can I show the class how to do a pirouette?" she asked excitedly.

"I don't think so, dear. You might hurt yourself," Ms. Hitchings replied starchily as Olivia slumped back to her seat.

Kaleb announced that he liked the color black, all kinds of magic, math and card tricks and rodents of all kinds "especially rats." When Kaleb reached around to pull something out of his back pocket, Ms. Hitchings' eyes grew wide, as if she thought a rat might appear right there in the classroom.

But it was just a deck of cards.

"I know some really cool tricks," Kaleb offered.

"I don't think that will be necessary Kaleb, nor appropriate," Ms. Hitchings said, relief showing on her face.

Next, it was Rudy's turn. Standing tall at the front of

the room, he quickly ran through his list.

"I like science, puzzles, mysteries, and all kinds of candy," he said, starting to walk back to his seat. "Oh, and I like Mr. J."

Ms. Hitchings made the slightest of harrumphing sounds and called Grace's name.

Grace walked slowly to the front of the room and turned to face the class. Taking a blue index card out of her jeans pocket, she glanced down at what she'd written and then began speaking in a clear, calm voice.

"One of the things people need to know about me is that I am always honest and fair, and I expect other people to treat me the same way." Grace turned to Ms. Hitchings. "If you want me to always compliment you or say 'yes' without thinking about it, then you've come to the wrong person."

Rudy elbowed B. "Cool, huh?"

But B wasn't paying too much attention. He was starting to think maybe he should change some of his fun facts. Then Grace looked right at him and something changed. B knew she could tell he was nervous. He saw her glance down at her index card, then up at him again. The whole class sat waiting for her second fun fact.

Then Grace did something no one understood at first, especially Ms. Hitchings. Grace ripped her blue index card in half, then in half again, and again. It made a satisfying *scritch-scratch* sound. Then she tossed the pieces into the trashcan. Little pieces of blue paper fluttered like birds near Ms. Hitchings' feet.

"Grace?" Ms. Hitchings asked.

"That's pretty much all you need to know about me," Grace said. "But I have some fun facts I can tell you about someone else."

She looked right at B and smiled a big smile.

"B is my friend, and the first fun fact you need to know about him is that he likes to be called B. *Not* Blaine. *Not* Blaine Powell. Just B."

"Fun Fact #2: B likes to cook, and he bakes the best cupcakes anywhere in Southern California. If you're nice, maybe he'll give you one." Grace looked at Ms. Hitchings as if this was definitely not a possibility.

"Fun Fact # 3: B has lots of friends here at New Horizons, and nobody *ever* made fun of him, until a certain school year began."

"This really isn't what—," Ms. Hitchings began.

"Fun Fact # 4: B knows all there is to know about birds and butterflies. Just ask him."

B felt himself blushing and kept his eyes fixed on his pink sneakers.

"Fun Fact #5:" Grace continued, "And this is the most important one. B is a boy. He likes to wear pink and he doesn't want any trouble about it."

Then without so much as a glance in Ms. Hitchings' direction, Grace walked proudly back to her seat and a thunderous round of applause filled Room 2A.

Chapter 4:
Halloween Fun

B's parents were no-nonsense kind of folks. They didn't make their children special meals.

They expected B and Patti-Anne to help out around the house without always being asked.

And they had long ago decided that the best way to raise their children was to present them with a whole range of good options, let them choose, and hope they learned from any mistakes.

So when B came home from school and told his parents what Grace had done in class during Five Fun Facts Day, they were pleased but they both took it in stride.

"Maybe we should make Grace your press agent," B's mother said, smiling and giving B a hug. "And she's right, you know. You *can* be whoever you want to be."

B's father was a bit more practical. "At least invite her over for cookies and milk," he laughed.

B knew it was easy for parents to say don't worry, just be yourself, but he wondered if they knew how hard that really was.

This became very clear one day in late October.

Ms. Hitchings had just finished demonstrating how snakes shed their skin. Normally, this would have been a pretty exciting topic. Everyone had hoped to see a *real* snake and *real* snakeskin. Instead, Ms. Hitchings brought out a stuffed green snake with a zippered outer skin. Once she'd unzipped it and pulled out a skinny yellow snake from inside, the rest of the lesson was pretty boring—until she said something that got the whole class listening.

"Now then, children, Halloween is coming up, and although it is not necessarily a holiday of which I approve," she sniffed, "What with all that candy passing hands, it does have some positive features."

B sat up straighter, listening. Halloween was B's favorite holiday. On Halloween, B had discovered you could be whatever you wanted to be, and no one made fun of you—not even the grown-ups. Instead, they *ooh'ed* and *ahh'ed* and handed out tasty treats.

"This year," Ms. Hitchings continued, "Instead of dressing up like goblins and witches, I want you to think a little differently. Some of you may have an idea of what you want to be when you grow up. Would anyone like to share?"

Twenty hands shot into the air. Ms. Hitchings pointed to a small boy in the front row. "Yes, Duane?"

"I—I," Duane lowered his hand and jiggled in his seat. "I forgot," he said quietly.

"Ah. I see. All right. Anyone else? Anika?"

Anika, who was taller and heavier than any other kid in Room 2A, stood up. "I want to be a singer," she said proudly, tossing her long hair over one shoulder.

"Hmmm. That might be a wee bit hard to demonstrate in a costume, but you might consider an opera singer. They are usually quite large people," Ms. Hitchings announced as Anika sank heavily back into her chair.

One by one, the kids in Room 2A called out their hopes and dreams and each one braced themselves for Ms. Hitchings' response.

"An artist!"

"That should be easy...just wear your oldest clothes," Ms. Hitchings chuckled.

"A vet!"

"Messy!" Ms. Hitchings wrinkled up her nose. "And smelly."

"Video game designer!"

"Goodness! Do we really need more of those distractions?"

"Vibration expert!"

"Ahhm—," Ms. Hitchings said, stumped.

B had an idea of what he wanted to be when he grew up too, but he kept his hands folded in his lap as the class buzzed with excitement. This time, everyone would have to wait for him to show them.

"Alright class, that's enough for now. Remember you don't need to decide right away."

The bell rang and Ms. Hitchings handed Rudy a piece of paper. "Rudy, on your way out would you drop this off in the office, please?"

That night B and his family went out to dinner at Temple Garden, their favorite Chinese restaurant. After the waiter had brought the tiny tray of fortune cookies, B told them about Ms. Hitchings' Halloween assignment.

"Mom...do you think...maybe just this once, I could look through Patti-Anne's closet? Please?"

His mother paused, thinking. B snuck a glance across the table. Patti-Anne cracked open her cookie and scowled.

"It's up to your sister," she said finally. "But—," His mother hesitated. She bent closer to B and put her arm over his shoulder. "You love to cook. We could find you a white jacket and chef's hat. Wouldn't that be easier? It doesn't matter if it's not your honest-to-goodness absolutely true-blue wish."

Now it was B's turn to hesitate. He's already thought about dressing up like an ornithologist by wearing his bird-watching vest and bringing his binoculars. He could tell the class about some of the cool things he knew about birds, like how hummingbirds can fly backwards, or how butterflies can't fly at all if it's too cold outside. But...that didn't seem right anymore.

"It does matter," he finally whispered.

Patti-Anne crunched loudly on her cookie. "He's right," she said. "It does."

B looked up, surprised at his sister's unexpected show of support.

Patti-Anne just shrugged. "I guess Halloween's as good a time as any. Here," she said, tossing him a cookie.

B cracked the cookie in half, then slipped out the thin white piece of paper. He stared hard at the printing. A couple of the words were tricky.

"What's it say?" he asked, handing it back.

"You are permitted to invent your life," Patti-Anne read aloud. Then she laughed.

Knowing that he had to eat the cookie to make it come true, B popped both halves in his mouth, smiling as he ate.

"You're my hero," B's mother said, giving him a hug.

• • •

IT
DOES
MATTER

The following Friday, the day of Room 2A's Halloween party, B got up extra early to be sure he had enough time to get dressed and ready. The night before, he'd chosen yellow tights and a black leotard and Patti-Anne's twirly yellow and black skirt that she had used for figure skating but couldn't fit into anymore.

"Honey, I really think I should drive you to school today..." Mom said, watching him get ready, "And maybe stay for a bit."

B ignored her. He knew his mother was worried but he wanted to do this himself.

When he was finished, as a final touch he wrapped a fluffy pink feather boa around his neck and pouffed up his hair until it almost floated.

"Just don't wreck my stuff," Patti-Anne warned as they hopped off the bus, but when B looked at her she was smiling. "Have fun!"

She gave him a hug and ran across the playground to her friends just as Rudy sprinted up, dressed all in black with two antenna-like spikes coming out of his head.

"What are you supposed to be?" B laughed. "I thought you wanted to be a doctor."

"Shh, it's a secret," Rudy said. "You'll see."

A few kids stared as B walked by, but everybody was so excited about their own costumes that nobody paid too much attention.

Inside, Grace met up with them smiling. "You look lovely," she said, fluffing B's skirt.

"Yeah," Rudy grinned as they filed into the classroom. "I can't wait to see what the parents think about your get-up."

Parents!

B had been so focused on making sure his own parents didn't insist on chaperoning him that he's forgotten Ms. Hitchings had invited *all* of Room 2A's parents to the party! He slowed his steps. Parents always made things more complicated....what would they think about his costume? With Rudy's words echoing in his head, he started to sweat.

"Alright, let's begin." Ms. Hitchings called to the class. "Who would like to be first?"

Rudy rushed to raise his hand, winking at B.

"And you are?" Ms. Hitchings asked.

"An entomologist who studies *Gromphadorhina portentosa*," Rudy said. "You know what that is, right?"

"Oh! Yes, yes, of course," Ms. Hitchings stammered and the class tittered. "How clever."

Visiting parents began arriving. They waved to their children and lined up along the back wall, whispering amongst themselves. B shifted in his seat, waiting his turn.

The room was hot and crowded and there wasn't even any candy to make it better. No one had really and truly believed that Ms. Hitchings wouldn't allow any candy at the Halloween party, but she proved them wrong. She'd even collected it from some startled parents.

"Kaleb, why don't you go next?" Ms. Hitchings said.

Kaleb was dressed all in brown, and a long tail dragged along the floor behind him as he walked slowly up to the front of the classroom.

Ms. Hitchings looked Kaleb up and down, then lowered her one eyebrow. "Kaleb? Please explain."

Kaleb stared at Ms. Hitchings. "I like monkeys," he said in a quiet voice.

"Well...that's all very well and good, but your costume was supposed to represent something you might want to be when you grow up. I don't think you want to grow up to be a moneky, do you?"

Kaleb's eyes grew wide. Then he smiled a big smile. "That would be awesome!" he cried, jumping up and down and swinging his tail around wildly.

Ms. Hitchings sighed a loud sigh. "Very well, Kaleb, that's enough. Next, please."

She waved to Grace to come forward.

Grace's costume consisted of a big aluminum arch that swept over her head. "I'm going to be a roller coaster designer," Grace announced. To keep her costume from collapsing, she had to walk very slowly and keep extra straight.

Ms. Hitchings frowned. "I think that might be a better job for one of the boys in the class."

Grace rolled her eyes and let out a big sigh. She did an about-face and sat down so hard in her seat the upper track over her head came crashing down to the floor.

Now it was B's turn.

He stood up and turned to face the wall of visiting parents. A wave of murmurs and some giggles rolled over him as everyone took in his costume. He gulped. Then, just as he was about to begin, he heard it—

"That's sooo gay!"

Whoever whispered it—was it one of the *parents?*— did in that way that meant they really wanted you to hear it.

And B did hear it. Loud and clear.

Grace tried to catch his eye and offer support, but this time she couldn't help him. It was too late.

"Blaine Powell, please explain your costume to us," he heard Ms. Hitchings say.

But he couldn't explain. Not to Ms. Hitchings. Not to the roomful of murmuring parents standing and watching him with arms folded across their chests, their eyes full of questions. He couldn't tell them who he really wanted to be when he grew up. He just didn't know how.

Then he remembered his fortune cookie—

Invent. You are permitted to invent your life.

So B lied.

"I—I'm a bird. A rosy-finch." He tugged nervously at his pink boa. "They're really colorful. I want to grow up to be..." He stopped. "I mean...I want to study birds."

Then B hurried back to his seat, trying his hardest not to cry. He was smart enough to know when you're a seven-year old boy dressed up like a girl, you'd better not make things any worse by crying.

Chapter 5:
The Uncooperative Phase

After the disastrous Halloween party, B felt so ashamed and nervous he didn't want to go to school again at all.

He'd let Rudy and Grace down.

He'd let his family down, especially Patti-Anne.

Most of all, he'd let himself down.

B felt so bad that he hadn't told the truth about his costume that when Monday arrived, he faked a stomach-ache and Mom let him stay home from school. On Tuesday, he added a headache. On Wednesday he added a cold and his mother grew suspicious. B had to remember to cough really, really loud every few minutes.

But by Thursday he'd run out of things that could be making him sick.

"How about home schooling?" B pleaded. "Just think of all the fun stuff we could do together!"

Mom wasn't buying it. She sat down on his bed with a sigh. "What happened that's making you want to stay home from school all week?"

Tired of pretending, B told his mother everything that had been going on in Ms. Hitchings' class ever since school started in September.

He told her about how he couldn't use the big, private bathroom near the art room.

He told her how Ms. Hitchings insisted on calling him "Blaine Powell," not "B."

And he told her how he hadn't been brave enough to explain his Halloween costume.

It felt good to tell his mother all these things, but by the time he finished they were both crying.

"We'll get to the bottom of this, B...I promise," Mom said, rocking him back and forth. "And you need to promise you'll tell me when things like this happen again."

B didn't like seeing his mother so sad, so he promised, even though he wasn't sure he could always keep his word.

• • •

On his first day back at school, B was still a little nervous, until he stepped into Room 2A and discovered Ms. Hitchings having some trouble of her own.

His teacher was standing just inside the doorway, talking to Miss Chin, the New Horizons principal. Miss Chin did not look happy.

Murmurs and rustlings swept over the curious students even though they could only catch a word here and there passing between the two women.

"How could— a mistake—not sure what to do...."

Ms. Hitchings stood wringing her hands, glancing

nervously at a white sheet of paper Ms. Chin was holding.

"What happened?" B asked Rudy, who was sure to know.

"Look!" Rudy pointed at the big insect tank on the shelf by the window. "The hissing cockroaches. She was supposed to order 4 ...but somehow, 40 arrived!"

"40?" B glanced over at the clear tank on the shelf. The cockroaches were *huge,* the biggest ones already about four inches long. The tank was so crowded some had to lie on top of others, while a few tried squeezing themselves into a hollowed out branch near the back.

HISS - SSSS-SSS!

"Ummm, Rudy, you wouldn't have any information on how that mistake happened, would you?" Grace asked, nudging B.

Rudy grinned. "Couldn't tell you....," he said, "All I did was deliver the order form to the office. Although, it did give me the idea to dress up as *Gromphadorhina portentosa*."

At that, the three friends started to laugh so hard it was a good thing Ms. Hitchings was otherwise occupied. For the whole rest of the year, B couldn't look at the cockroaches without smiling, imagining what Ms. Hitchings face must have looked like when she first opened the package.

Later that morning, during lunch break, Rudy came rushing up to Grace and B and announced more news— he'd overheard that a new kid would be joining Room 2A.

Sure enough, the very next day, Mia arrived, in a special taxicab because the school bus system couldn't figure out any other way to get her from her house to New Horizons. The whole first day, all she bragged about was how she'd ordered the driver around, even though no one really believed her.

With the whole playground watching, Mia stepped out of the cab wearing purple shorts and sunglasses, even though it wasn't very sunny out, and a frilly white lace blouse and orange sweater. But what B noticed more than anything was the doll she carried in her arms. It was the biggest, fanciest doll he had ever seen.

He couldn't resist. Without really thinking what he was doing, he walked right up to Mia.

"Your doll looks just like you," B said, staring. And it did. It was dressed in an outfit just like Mia's with the same green eyes and curly brown hair.

"Wow....what a genius," Mia replied, rolling her eyes.

"Can I see?" B asked, reaching out, but Mia clutched her doll closer and took a step back. B could feel Mia looking him up and down, examining his long red hair, pink sneakers and yellow sweatpants. Suddenly, he wished he'd picked out his striped flannel shirt to wear today.

"My brother says boys who play with dolls are sissies," Mia hissed.

B felt his face redden. "I – I don't want to play with your doll...I just want to see it."

But Mia had already brushed past him and was running across the playground, yelling. "Ha-ha-ha! He asked to play with my doll! What a SISSY!"

Room 2A soon learned that Mia had her own special way of doing things. Right from the start, it was clear that she seemed to have missed the cooperative phase.

Instead of walking around kids, she pushed them out of her way.

Instead of talking, Mia just complained. That first day alone, she complained about the cubbies, the circle rug on the floor, the playground equipment, and the lunch lady.

And of course, she complained about Ms. Hitchings.

Every day, while Ms. Hitchings gave her lessons, Mia would sit scowling, mumbling awful, mean things under her breath. But the strangest thing happened. Whenever Ms. Hitchings spoke to Mia, she somehow managed to transform herself into a different person, smiling and answering Ms. Hitchings' questions politely.

So Ms. Hitchings never seemed to notice there were two Mias.

One day, about a week after Mia arrived, the class was outside in the playground at break time. Mia had been mean to almost everyone all morning, muttering little comments under her breath if they missed a word in reading, teasing other kids about the lunch they'd brought. Now Mia walked right up to Falak who was sitting on the low wall near the swings, reading a book.

Falak was Muslim and had come to New Horizons School at the very end of last year. She was so quiet and so timid that B had hardly gotten to know her at all. She didn't know English very well so she hardly said a word in class and she never, ever played with other kids.

"Why do you always wear that stupid scarf?" B heard

Mia ask Falak in a loud voice.

"Is mine," Falak whispered, barely raising her eyes.

Everyone in the playground stopped what they were doing and turned to watch. Mia stood looming over Falak, holding her doll clone that she carried with her everywhere.

"Yeah, I know it's yours...but why do you always wear it? It looks dumb."

A hush fell over the playground. Nobody moved. Nobody knew what to say. Nobody had ever known anyone quite as bossy and mean as Mia.

B didn't totally understand why Falak dressed the way she did either, but it didn't matter. He knew it had something to do with her religion and that was enough. He hadn't thought much more about it.

Until now.

Now all he could think about was how Falak must be feeling. B knew exactly what it felt like to be laughed and stared at and he didn't like it one bit. He felt himself getting warm. Then he felt really, really hot. He saw Falak shake her head. Then she slinked off to a corner of the playground and slumped down onto a bench. Mia quickly followed.

And maybe because none of it had anything at all to do with him, B turned and marched straight across the playground towards Mia.

"Don't be such a bully!" he yelled, as he got closer.

B never, ever shouted, but today he did. Mia whirled around towards him, scowling. B felt like punching her, making her feel as bad as she had made Falak feel....as bad as he felt when people called him names.

"Oooh, is she your girlfriend?" Mia teased, laughing. "No, wait...*that* can't be right!"

Ms. Hitchings and some other teachers had come out to the playground and were running towards them. B's parents had taught him to breath deeply and count to 10 when he was feeling angry.

He tried it now. He counted to 10.

Nothing happened. Then he counted to 20...then 30...

Mia stood there grinning at him like she owned the world. B knew what he was about to do was wrong, but he did it anyway. Reaching out, he pulled Mia's precious doll from her arms and flung it as far as he could across the playground. He heard a loud scraping sound as the doll fell with a twack and slid across the asphalt.

Mia stared at him, shocked, her eyes and mouth wide open. Then she started to cry.

B ignored her. He closed his eyes, took a deep breath, and turned around, ready to face the oncoming army of teachers. He knew he was in big trouble.

Still, throwing that doll had felt good. Almost as good as seeing Mia cry.

CHAPTER 6:
GROMPHADORHINA PORTENTOSA

After B's fight with Mia, everything in Room 2A seemed to change.

B was given two punishments for ruining her doll. Apparently, the thing had scraped its face so badly it was no longer an exact replica of Mia and had to be replaced. With one week to go before winter break, Ms. Hitchings made B stay inside and clean up the classroom at playground recess. His parents, who sympathized but still disapproved of his choice, gave him extra chores at home and made him promise to be nice to Mia when school started again in January.

B knew he should feel more sorry about what he'd done, but he couldn't. Mia was just too mean for him to care. Second grade was turning out so badly that B was dreading the return to classes in January before winter break had even begun.

"Sometimes, good comes out of the worse situations," Mom said, trying to cheer him up.

"Everybody needs a little kindness," Dad added.

But B didn't feel like being kind.

Not to Ms. Hitchings.

Not to Mia's stupid doll.

And certainly not to Mia, who had made it very clear that she didn't like him at all.

Over winter break, B's mother put her campaign against Ms. Hitchings into full swing. She made phone calls, sent out e-mails and organized all the other parents she knew at New Horizons School. By the time everyone had compared stories, no one could imagine how Ms. Hitchings had ever been hired in the first place. Still, the school staff was so busy with children who had allergies, children who couldn't eat certain foods, or children who could only eat certain foods, that following up on Ms. Hitchings' rules wasn't their first priority.

So because he couldn't trust himself yet, B decided to stay as far away from Mia as possible when school started again in January.

But Mia had other plans.

Almost from the very first day back, instead of being mad at B and avoiding him, Mia always seemed to be hanging around. She watching everything he did, seemed to follow him everywhere, even copied his projects! Once, when the class was making paper decorations for Martin Luther King Jr. Day, B saw her sneaking looks at his artwork. Then she made the same wreath he had— *exactly*—filled with cut-out silhouettes of different kinds of birds!

Of course, Ms. Hitchings loved Mia's wreath. That afternoon, on the way to recess, B quickly crumpled his up and tossed it in the recycling.

Another day, at reading time, B raised his hand to say he wanted to do a book report on "Junie B. Jones and a Little Monkey Business."

Mia waved her hand in the air frantically. "Oh-oh, Ms. Hitchings?" she said, not waiting to be called on. "I'm afraid that's not possible. I've already picked out the same book first. See?" Mia held up a copy of another old paperback book in her desk and Ms. Hitchings couldn't or wouldn't see the difference. Mia was assigned the Junie B. Jones book.

And when Ms. Hitchings asked B to feed the hissing cockroaches, Mia's hand shot up in the air again.

"I can help him, Ms. Hitchings. I know all about insects."

B froze halfway up in his chair.

"Aw, jeez," Rudy sighed.

"I'm not sure he needs help Mia, but thank you so

much for your generosity," Ms. Hitchings crooned.

"Oh, he needs help. Cockroaches can be very finicky. I even know the zoological name for cockroaches. Do you want to know what it is?"

"No!" Grace said loudly and the class snickered.

"*Gromphadorhina portentosa*," Rudy murmured under his breath.

"It's *Gromphadorhina portentosa*," Mia said anyway. "They're called hissing cockroaches because they force air through the pores on their stomachs."

"Grophohorra...," Ms. Hitchings repeated, glancing at Rudy as if she was trying to recall a very important memory. "Ah, yes, well, that's very impressive, Mia," she said, giving up. "Your parents must be very proud of you."

B had been looking right at Mia, trying hard to figure out what she was up to, so he saw it happen. At the mention of her parents, Mia's expression changed. Just for a few seconds, she seemed to lose her toughness. It was like all the air had been taken out of the Mia balloon and B was the only one who saw it.

"Why don't you go on then and help Blaine Powell," Ms. Hitchings continued. " The rest of you, please take out your counting books."

B and Mia stood side by side, dropping lettuce leaves into the top of the cockroaches' tank in silence.

51

"Why are you always hanging around me," B finally whispered. "I know you don't like me."

By now, Mia had recovered and was back to her mean old self.

"To keep an eye on you, I guess," she grinned.

"What's that supposed to mean?"

Mia shrugged and headed back to her desk. B sighed and glanced up at the big calendar that hung at the front of the room.

Spring break was eight long weeks away.

• • •

One windy day in March, Ms. Hitchings had just finished explaining poison snakebites to the class when Miss Chin knocked and walked into the room. It was always special and exciting whenever the principal came into the classroom, and all twenty of Room 2A's fidgeting students sat up a little straighter.

Ms. Hitchings, on the other hand, looked like she was going to shout the principal out of the room. Ms. Hitching did not like anyone to interrupt her lessons.

But Miss Chin didn't seem to notice.

"I thought I would just check one last time to be sure none of your students have changed their minds about trying out." She smiled at the class and waved a thin sheet of paper in the air.

B caught Rudy's eye, wondering if he knew what as going on but Rudy just shrugged.

"No aspiring thespians here?"

Grace's hand shot up. "Miss Chin, I don't think we understand."

"Why, the play!" Miss Chin said, looking puzzled. "Room 2A is the only classroom where no one has signed up to audition for the Spring play. I thought I'd double check one last time before—,"

"*What!?*" Grace shouted, jumping up out of her seat.

Miss Chin stopped. The whole class stared at her with wide eyes.

"Ms. Hitchings?" Miss Chin turned slowly away from the students. "Haven't you spoken to your class about the Spring play? I asked *all* teachers to make the announcement daily for the last *two weeks.*"

Ms. Hitchings stood stock-still against the chalkboard as a low murmur rippled through the room.

"Ms. Hitchings?" Miss Chin repeated.

"Didn't see the need...," Ms. Hitchings mumbled, as if she was talking to herself. "Frivolous activity...No purpose, really..."

Miss Chin's face got redder and redder until B thought it would turn purple. She shot Ms. Hitchings one last glance, heaved a huge sigh, then turned back to address the roomful of excited students.

"Children, next month grades 1 through 3 will be presenting New Horizons' annual Spring play. Everyone is invited to audition if you would like to participate. We'll be performing "Our Underwater Friends." SO PLEASE...," Miss Chin raised her voice to be heard over the wave of excitement that had taken hold of the class, "...COME WITH ME NOW IF YOU'RE INTERESTED."

Miss Chin had hardly finished her announcement when half a dozen kids shot out of their seats and rushed up to the front of the room.

B loved plays. Even more important, he was pretty sure a play with a title like "Our Underwater Friends" would have mermaids in it. Mermaids were his absolute favorite.

But as he got up to join the others, he remembered Mia. He snuck a look behind to where she sat, but he needn't have bothered. Mia waved back at him, grinning.

Mia, of course, would be joining the auditions, too.

Chapter 7:
Mermaids and Starfish

B rushed down the hallway, desperate to get as far away from Mia as he could.

But Mia was persistent. She stayed right there beside B, stuck to him like glue.

"What are you going to try out for?" she hissed in his ear. "A mermaid?"

It was as if she'd read his mind. Rattled, he ignored her and pushed his way forward to catch up with Rudy and Grace.

"Can you believe she never told us?" Grace fumed as they scrambled into the auditorium and flopped down to wait. "That's just wrong."

"How did I miss this?" Rudy said, scowling. He kicked at the back of the empty seat in front of him with the toe of his sneaker. "She almost got away with it, too."

"Maybe it's good in a way," Grace, always the optimist, said. "Maybe she won't be able to talk her way out of this one."

B sat listening to Rudy and Grace but inside he was buzzing with excitement. If there was a mermaid in the play, he knew for sure he wanted to audition for the role. There was just one small problem. He snuck a glance behind him to where Mia sat. Sure enough, there she was, staring back at him with a devilish grin on her face. *Arrrgh.*

B quickly looked away.

Up on the stage Miss Chin and Mr. Ross, the art teacher, were setting up rows of chairs next to a long table. Everyone talked and squirmed in their seats, anxious to get started.

Tap-tap-tap. Mr. Ross checked the microphone to be sure it was working.

"Welcome everyone," Mr. Ross greeting the sea of children. "I can see you're all just as excited as I am to be here, so let me begin by telling you all about "Our Underwater Friends."

Then, because Mr. Ross was an artist, he explained how the sea was a magical, wondrous place filled with incredible plants and creatures, each with their own special story to tell.

"We need a special actress to play the role of the undersea Mermaid who leads the sea creatures," Mr. Ross said, smiling out at the crowded room. "So if any young lady out there thinks she's good at memorizing and might be interested, please come see me."

The room erupted with cheers and clapping.

Mr. Ross raised his voice, "But no worries. There's a role for everyone who wants to be in the play."

Rudy leaned towards B. "Yeah, right," he whispered. "Being a guppy is the same as being the star."

"We need lots of guppies and starfish and squid and octopuses to make this show happen," Mr. Ross continued. "So don't be shy...c'mon up here!"

Rudy gave B an "I-told-you-so" look.

B slumped down in his seat. Mr. Ross was looking for "a special actress" to play the role of the Mermaid. He had no chance.

For the next hour, everyone trooped up onto the stage and demonstrated how they could swim like a guppy, make *glup-glup* sounds like a fish, twirl like a starfish, or sway like a sea anemone. B waited patiently, the last one in line behind a small group of possible mermaids, including Mia who pranced and danced for Mr. Ross.

Watching Mia audition, B heart sank. He had to admit she sounded pretty good when she repeated Mr. Ross's lines.

Finally, after Lily and Becca, it was B's turn. But Mr. Ross, thinking he was finished, stood up and tucked his clipboard under his arm. B didn't budge.

"Yes?" Mr. Ross said, blinking.

"I want to try out for the part of the Mermaid," B said bravely.

"But—you're a *boy*...aren't you?"

B nodded. He and Mr. Ross stared at each other. He could feel everyone watching them again, but this time he planted his feet right where he was and waited.

B wanted to tell Mr. Ross that it was okay to like girl things better than boy things and still be a boy. He wanted to point out that Becca, who had just gone ahead of him, had short hair and was a girl. Did her short hair make her less of a girl?

Mr. Ross was an artist. He should have known better.

The minutes ticked away. Finally, B couldn't stand it any more.

"I'm—I'm pretty good at memorizing lines," he said.

"Well—alright then," Mr. Ross said, sitting back down. "I suppose there's no reason why you can't try for the part. Let's see what you can do."

Chapter 8:
Our Underwater Friends

"You WHAT?" Patti-Anne screamed, her mouth full of spaghetti and meatballs. Her fork landed on her plate with a clatter. "They'll eat you alive!"

It was dinner time and B had casually announced that he'd auditioned for the part of the Mermaid in the Spring play. Flustered, B looked to Mom and Dad for guidance.

"Patti-Anne, let's hear the whole story first...," Mom said, but B noticed her eyebrows turning downward, always a sure sign that she was worried.

"I'm serious, Mom, he's got to think about what this means," Patti-Anne said to her parents as if B wasn't there. "Why does he always have to put himself out there in the world like that?"

"He wants to be himself," Dad said. "Imagine what it would be like if we told you couldn't play on the soccer team because you're a girl."

"That's not the same thing," Patti-Anne argued, pushing her plate away. "He doesn't need to be a *mermaid* in the play...he could be a...a fish...or an eel. Something else. Something—,"

Patti-Anne stopped herself, catching B's eye.

"Something what?" he asked.

"Something...normal," Patti-Anne mumbled, looking away.

"Honey," Mom said softly, reaching across the table to pat Patti-Anne's arm. "This *is* normal—for B.

Patti-Anne pulled her hand away. She stood up, pushing her chair back from the table. It made an awful scraping sound. "Yeah, well, don't say I didn't warn you if something happens."

B watched as Patti-Anne stalked out of the kitchen, his own plate of food growing cold. Maybe Patti-Anne was right. B hadn't thought that far ahead. He didn't know what would happen if he got the part. The memory of Halloween flashed through his mind.

Maybe he *would* get eaten alive, just like Patti-Anne said. But maybe he wouldn't. Butterflies used all kinds of tricks to keep from being eaten. Maybe he could be like a butterfly! It was only acting, after all, right?

At least that's what B told himself.

They'll Eat You Alive!

The next morning, the playground was empty as the buses arrived and everyone rushed inside to check the cast list that Mr. Ross had said would be posted. B scrambled off the bus with Rudy and Grace. Together they hurried down the ramp that led to the art room. B's heart thumped in his chest as everyone jostled for space.

"Hey, I'm an octopus!" Kaleb announced. "Cool!"

"Oooo...we're both dancing seaweed!" two girls squealed and hugged.

"Grace—you're the narrator!" B heard Rudy say. "I'm a clownfish—not bad!"

B craned his neck to see the thin sheet of white paper taped to the wall beside the door. Mia had elbowed her way through the crowd too, and stood behind him now, breathing down his neck.

Suddenly, she screeched in his ear.

"Yes!! I'm the Mermaid! I've been picked for the Mermaid!"

B closed his eyes. When he opened them again, he ran his finger down the list looking for his own name—

There it was. B. Browning.

He had wished with all his heart to play the part of the Mermaid. Instead, he'd been cast as a starfish.

B didn't want to be a starfish.

There were other kids who could be starfish, or

guppies, or seaweed. All of his worrying had been for nothing. He had wanted to be the Mermaid and if he couldn't be her—well, then he didn't want to be in the play at all.

And there was nothing Rudy or Grace could say to change his mind.

• • •

Even after B made his decision, being at school felt awful. It seemed like everyone except B was busy practicing for the play, rehearsing their lines, their dances, or their songs. B knew it wasn't true, but that's what it felt like. Even Falak had been persuaded to participate—she was going to be a manta ray.

For the whole next month, B sulked, feeling sorry for himself.

And something else happened that was odd. Once Mia had beat B out for the part of the Mermaid, she was nicer to him than she'd ever been before.

She stopped teasing him about the clothes he wore.

She stopped following him around and smirking.

Once, he even thought he saw her smiling at him from across the room.

Then one afternoon, B happened to come in early from playground recess to find Mia sitting at her desk practicing her lines. He could tell she was concentrating hard. He watched her stare at the sheet of white paper on her desk, then scrunch her eyes closed, her lips moving as she tried to memorize the words. B stepped quietly towards his desk, pretending not to notice or care.

But Mia heard him and looked up.

"I can't do it," she groaned. "It's too hard!"

B nodded, nervous, not sure if she was faking or not.

She sighed again, louder this time, and tapped the eraser end of her pencil on her desk.

"I need help…I can't do this all by myself. Some of these words are *hard*. Mr. Ross said he would help, but he's always so busy. He expects me to memorize all this!

Mia waved her thick stack of paper in the air.

I NEED HELP!

B shifting uncomfortably in his seat, wondering what Mia expected him to do about it. Suddenly Mia's face brightened.

"Hey!" she said, breaking into a big smile, "You could help me practice! I bet I'd learn these stupid lines way faster if I had a partner."

B's mouth opened but nothing came out.

Help Mia learn the lines for the part that he wished was his?

"So? What do you think?" Mia asked again, waiting. "Will you help?"

B swallowed hard and kept his eyes on his sneakers. He remembered his parents telling him to try to be nicer to Mia.

"Why can't you study at home....with your parents or something?"

Mia burst out laughing. "That's a joke! My parents are so busy, no way would they help."

"What are they so busy doing?" B looked at Mia, surprised. Parents *always* helped, didn't they?

But Mia wasn't smiling or laughing anymore.

"Arguing," she said angrily. "That's all they ever do."

B didn't know what to say. He watched as Mia fussed with her stack of papers. Suddenly, she crumpled them all up into a ball and threw it hard, across the room towards the wastepaper basket.

"Never mind," Mia said, slumping down in her seat. "I get it. Why would you want to help me?"

B tried to think of something to say to make Mia feel better, but he couldn't. That's what parents were for. To notice when things went wrong and you were sad.

Why, just last night, B had felt so sad he couldn't fall asleep. He lay in his bed in his dark room for what seemed like hours, thinking that maybe everyone was right.

Maybe he should just cut his hair, and start wearing plain old blue jeans and white shirts and white sneakers.

He'd felt so sad and confused he'd even climbed out of his warm bed and sat crouched on the floor of his closet. Patti-Anne's yellow and black skirt—the one he'd worn for the Halloween disaster—hung above, brushing against his shoulders.

For what seemed like hours, B thought and thought about what he could to fix things. But all the thinking had made him sad, just as sad as Mia looked now, and finally his eyes felt heavy with sleep.

When he woke up this morning, he was surprised to find himself back in his own bed.

Could it be that Mia was as mean as she was to make up for feeling sad?

If that was true, then B *had* to help. Then maybe just

this once, Mia's parents would notice and she wouldn't have to feel so sad.

B got up, walked across the room and picked up Mia's crumpled balls of paper. Then he sat down in the chair next to Mia and smoothed them out as best he could.

Later, when B told Rudy and Grace he'd agreed to help Mia learn her lines, they both thought it was a really bad idea.

"She's just using you," Rudy told him. "See if she doesn't."

But B had made up his mind. So every day, instead of going outside for playground recess, B and Mia stayed inside Room 2A and worked on memorizing her two speeches. B still wasn't sure he liked Mia very much, but after what she told him about her parents, it didn't seem so hard to be nice to her anymore.

Chapter 9:
B in the World

Ms. Hitchings was never the same after the day Miss Chin scolded her for hiding the Spring play auditions from Room 2A.

Now instead of being just plain mean, she barked at kids for hardly any reason at all. Rudy had even seen her walking down the hallway mumbling to herself and scribbling notes on a napkin.

Then one day, Grace noticed something especially odd when she pulled out her spelling book to begin studying for a quiz.

"Hey! What's this?" she said. "Somebody's been messing with my book. Look!"

Rudy and B scrambled over to see. As Grace flipped through the pages, B could see that certain words had been blackened out with marker.

"Lemme check mine," Rudy said, hurrying back to his desk. "Me too!" he announced.

"Check some more," Grace ordered. Quickly Rudy and Grace and B pulled out almost all of Room 2A's spelling books and discovered the same black marks in every single one.

"Wait a minute!" Rudy said, "It's the same words blacked out in all the books!"

"Can you tell what they were?" Grace asked.

"Wait!" B shouted, rummaging through his backpack, "I took mine home last night."

He opened his book to one of the marked-up pages.

"C....C.....candy!"

"Check page 24...under "F"," Rudy said.

"F....fun...funny," B read.

"How about under 'S'?" Grace asked. They compared the two books.

"Soda," B whispered.

"Only one person could have done this," Rudy said. The three friends nodded.

"Ms. Hitchings," they said in unison.

"She crossed out everything she hates...," Grace whispered.

"Really weird..." Rudy shook his head.

And B and Rudy and Grace didn't want to think about what *that* might mean.

• • •

As the days ticked down to opening night of the Spring play, B was feeling more and more worried about Mia. With only two days to go before the big night, she was still having trouble with her lines.

70

"Oh, what's the difference?" Mia said angrily, crumbling up yet another copy of her lines and throwing to the floor, "It doesn't matter. Nobody's going to see it anyway."

"Sure they will," B said, trying to make Mia feel better. "The whole school will be there and all the teachers—,"

Mia's face drooped and she looked down. And that's how B knew. He knew Mia wasn't talking about just anybody seeing her performance. She was thinking about her parents.

B realized then that he had never seen Mia's parents at any of Room 2A's family events. Not even once. He'd never seen her being dropped off or picked up from school.

And he remembered that day months ago when she had sagged like a popped balloon when Ms. Hitchings mentioned how proud her parents must be.

"Are they coming?" he whispered, almost afraid to ask.

Mia shook her head.

"You don't need them there," B lied. "It'll be okay."

"Just because you don't need something," Mia said, wiping her eyes, "Doesn't mean you stop wanting it."

• • •

From then on, B couldn't stop thinking about Mia. So the night before the play, he decided to make a batch of cupcakes especially for her, lemon of course, but with bright green frosting in honor of Mia the Mermaid.

Friday night finally arrived. The auditorium was packed. It felt like the entire school was there, plus parents and grandparents, and teachers—everyone except Ms. Hitchings, who of course, would never dream of coming to a foolish play performance.

B slipped into his seat next to Patti-Anne and his parents, carefully placing his box of cupcakes on the floor near his feet. He looked around, wondering if maybe, at the last minute, Mia's parents had decided to come.

Grace was already up on the stage, ready to begin. When the lights went down, the whole room grew quiet and Grace spoke her opening lines into the microphone perfectly. Behind her, a school of bright golden guppies fluttered onto the stage, green and blue lights following them as they danced.

Then came the Coral Sisters—two third graders who sang a song about the beauty of the sea and how important it was to keep it clean so all the creatures could live.

B shifted in his seat, nervous. Mia's first lines came next, where she welcomed everyone to her underwater kingdom. B crossed his fingers, waiting for the Coral Sisters to finish their song.

Then Mia stepped out onto the stage, and the crowd gasped.

She wore a deep green leotard and long gown that sparkled in the stage lights. In one hand she carried a scepter and a golden crown balanced unsteadily on her head. B thought Mia looked beautiful, just like a real mermaid. And he only felt the slightest twinge of envy.

Carefully, Mia walked to the very front of the stage, her tail sweeping along behind her. She raised her head to face the audience, planted her scepter firmly on the ground, opened her mouth, and—

Nothing came out. Everyone waited.

"Greeting, humans, friends of the dwellers of the sea," B whispered in his seat.

Mia stood frozen, her mouth still open. Then, after what seemed like hours to B but must have really been only minutes, Mia turned and ran offstage—or shuffled really, because of her tight gown and tail.

"No!" B whispered.

"Serves her right," Patti-Anne said grumpily.

"The poor girl," B's mother said, shaking her head.

A buzz swept through the room as teachers, students, parents, and grandparents waited in the dark to see what would happen next.

What did happen, B never would have imagined, even in his wildest dreams. After an awkward minute or two, the lights came up and Mr. Ross walked out onto the stage.

"Folks, due to an unexpected situation," he said, "It seems we have a little change of plans. But fear not, the show will go on!" The audience tittered. "I've been told that there is another young actor in the audience who may be able to take over the role of the Mermaid. I'm told he knows all the lines."

B's eyes opened wide. He couldn't believe what he was hearing! Mia must have told Mr. Ross about practicing together.

"B? Are you out there?" Mr. Ross called out. "B. Browning?"

Everyone in the nearby rows swiveled their heads towards B.

"Don't do it!" Patti-Anne whispered. "They just want you now because they need you."

"Patti-Anne—," B's mother warned, "Let B make his own decision." She leaned over towards B. "Honey, what do you want to do?"

It was true what Mr. Ross said. He did know all the lines. He had wanted to get the part. But what Patti-Anne said was also true. Still….now that it was being offered to him….could he do it? He took a deep breath.

"I want to do it," he said, standing up.

The audience applauded as B walked towards the stage. Mr. Ross announced that intermission was coming

at the beginning of the play instead of in the middle so that B could have some time to change into his costume and get ready.

Thirty minutes later, Blaine Powell Browning, dressed in sparkly mermaid green, carrying a scepter and wearing a crown, delivered his lines flawlessly. The guppies fluttered, the eels and starfish danced, the Coral Sisters sang, and the anemones and seaweed swayed to the music.

The Spring play was a wondrous, fabulous, magical success.

And when it was over, the whole cast, including Mia, ate lemon cupcakes with green icing and gave B a rousing round of applause, thanking him for saving the show.

It was the best night of B's life, and his only wish was that he'd made *three times* as many cupcakes.

Chapter 10:
Our Civil Rights

After the excitement of Friday night, B felt like a star all weekend. He didn't think he could feel any happier—until Monday morning when he stepped off the bus.

"You'll never believe it!" Rudy yelled, running up to him on the playground. "C'mon! Follow me!"

B followed along, hurrying to keep up, wondering what could possibly have happened to create such a commotion. When he turned the corner of the hallway that led to his classroom, he stopped in his tracks, not quite believing what he was seeing.

"He's back!" Rudy laughed. 'Mr. J is back!"

There—pasted around the frame of the doorway

leading to Room 2A—were dozens of cut-out figures of Mickey Mouse.

"It's a miracle!" Grace announced, clapping her hands together. And when they stepped inside the room, it was true! Mr. J was back.

That whole first day, all the kids in Room 2A couldn't stop smiling. Hardly any schoolwork got done. Mr. J told them all about how he's been sick but was better now. He had been especially sorry to hear about the hard time they'd had with Ms. Hitchings.

"But that's all over now," he said, smiling. "And one of the first things we're going to do is go over the new rules of the classroom."

A few smiles faded, and the class grew quiet.

"It might seem easier, sometimes, to yell and boss somebody around rather than work things out. But that is not okay. It's not okay at home, on the playground, and it's definitely not okay in my class. Each of you is special, and we all need to respect each other."

Mr. J tacked up a big sheet of paper onto the front wall. "These are Room 2A's Civil Rights," he said. "And since I'm also going to be your teacher next year—," The class erupted in applause, "Let's go over them now."

Then Mr. J read aloud what he said were the five most important things they would ever learn in second grade.

Our Civil Rights . . .

I HAVE A RIGHT TO LEARN ABOUT MYSELF IN THIS ROOM.

This means that I will be free to express my opinions without being interrupted or punished.

I HAVE A RIGHT TO BE HAPPY AND TO BE TREATED WITH COMPASSION IN THIS ROOM.

This means that no one will laugh at me or hurt my feelings.

I HAVE A RIGHT TO BE MYSELF IN THIS ROOM.

This means that no one will treat me unfairly because I am different.

I HAVE A RIGHT TO HEAR AND BE HEARD IN THIS ROOM.

This means that we will listen when someone is talking. No one will yell, scream, shout, or make loud noises.

I HAVE A RIGHT TO BE SAFE IN THIS ROOM.

This means no one will hit, kick, push, hurt or bully me in any way.

When he finished reading, Mr. J passed out copies for everyone to keep and study.

The rest of the day flew by, and just before the dismissal bell rang, Mr. J announced that the end of the year sleepover was back on the schedule and everyone should start making plans for games and snacks.

"And make sure they're sweet, sugary snacks," he added, laughing.

As everyone scrambled towards the waiting buses, Mia stopped B on the playground.

"This is for you," she said, handing him an envelope.

B ripped the envelope open to find a hand-made thank you card inside, with a picture of a mermaid that Mia had drawn on the front.

"Read the inside," she said as Rudy and Grace came running up to see.

B opened the card.

"Thank you for helping me. Mostly, thank you for being who you are," B read aloud.

"Civil Right # 3," Grace said, smiling.

"Awesome," said Rudy, slapping B on the back.

On the way home, B thought about all the changes that had happened since school started in September. He had learned a lot, about himself and about other people. He thought hard about Civil Right # 3, too, and he was pretty sure being himself would always cause problems for some people.

People who thought he was just too different.

People who, like Mom said, "think you don't fit their cookie-cutter idea of what a boy or a girl should be."

But right now, sitting on the bus, laughing and talking with Rudy and Grace and Mia, it felt pretty perfect just being B in the world.

THE END

About the Author and Illustrator

Sharon Mentyka divides her time between design, teaching and writing for children. Her stories grow from small kernels of truth that explore common themes of fairness, transitions and helping the less powerful find their voice. She has had stories published in *ColumbiaKids*, *Cricket* and *Soundings Review*. Her experience as a member of a non-traditional family helped inspire "B in the World." See more about her writing projects at www.sharonmentyka.com

Stephen Schlott has been a graphic designer for over 20 years, with clients in both the private and non-profit sectors. He has illustrated projects for children, naturalists, communities, and museum visitors and embellishes many projects with his original photography and art. A proud gay father who embraces a non-traditional family, Stephen has been a Seattle LGBTQ leader serving gay fathers and their families for nearly 10 years. This is his first children's book.

Resources

Gender Spectrum
(510) 788-4412
email: info@genderspectrum.org
genderspectrum.org

Gender Spectrum provides education, training and support to help create a gender sensitive and inclusive environment for all children and teens.

Welcoming Schools Human Rights Campaign Foundation
(202) 628-4160
email: welcomingschools@hrc.org
welcomingschools.org

Welcoming Schools, a program of the Human Rights Campaign Foundation's Children, Youth and Families Program, is an LGBT-inclusive approach to addressing family diversity, gender stereotyping and bullying and name-calling in K-5 learning environments.

Gender Diversity
1-855-4GENDER
email: info@genderdiversity.org
genderdiversity.org

Gender Diversity increases the awareness and understanding of the wide range of gender variations in children, adolescents, and adults by providing family support, building community, increasing societal awareness, and improving the well-being for people of all gender identities and expressions.

Camp Ten Trees
(206) 288-9568
email: info@camptentrees.org

Camp Ten Trees is a loving and engaging youth camp environment for LGBTQ communities and their allies in Washington State. In addition to typical camp activities, campers engage in age-appropriate workshops exploring identity, issues of oppression/privilege, youth coalition building, social justice, and more.

STOMP Out Bullying
(877) 602-8559
stompoutbullying.org

STOMP Out Bullying is the leading national anti-bullying and cyberbullying organization for kids and teens in the U.S. They focus on reducing and preventing bullying, cyberbullying, and other digital abuse, and educating against homophobia, racism in schools, online and in communities across the country.

PACER's National Bullying Prevention Center
(888) 248-0822
email: bullying411@pacer.org
pacer.org/bullying

PACER's National Bullying Prevention Center actively leads social change so that bullying is no longer considered an accepted childhood rite of passage. They provide innovative resources for students, parents, educators and recognizes bullying as a serious community issue that impacts education, physical and emotional health, and the safety and well-being of students.

Acknowledgements

This book would not have been possible without the encouragement and help of many, many people to whom we owe my deepest thanks and appreciation.

Nancy Boutin and Pam Privett, for suggesting that a story like this was important to write.

My early readers for invaluable feedback and insights: Frances Wood, Stephanie Lile, Carmen Bernier Grand, Bonny Becker, Sara Crowe, Trudi Picciano, Karen Hirsch, Lupine Miller, Monica Ollson, Kirk Wheeler, Tracy Flynn and Elizabeth Ralston.

The 2nd graders at Broadview Thompson Elementary in Seattle and the Thursday afterschool kids at 826 Seattle. They enthusiastically said "yes" when asked if they would listen to chapters from a new book I was writing.Then they asked me to read more! Their questions helped solidify this book's characters and voice. Thanks, kids!

Karen Hirsch for all her guidance, encouragement and support.

The folks at GLAAD, Camp Ten Trees, Gender Spectrum, Gay Fathers Association of Seattle, Welcoming Schools, and Safe Schools Coalition Seattle for sharing vast amounts of information and resources to give this book a solid foundation and support network.

All my writer friends at the Northwest Institute for Literary Arts MFA program for their support, expertise, and tips.

Jennifer Finney Boylan for her inspirational writing and for tweeting and posting about this book.

Jodi Hall and Cupcake Royale for social media support and cupcakes!

Samuel Phillips-Corwin for his invaluable help with the video and Stephen Schlott for his gorgeous illustrations and elegant book design

To all our early supporters who gave this project the momentum to succeed. Thank you for helping bring B into the World!

Pamela Privett and
Helen Mendoza

Michael Poling

Camille Sata

_____

Nancy Boutin

Matt Brock

Nancy Megan Corwin

Bruce Gardner

Carol Mentyka

Kate B. Schlott

Abbe Wainwright and Jim Hill

Barbara Young

_____

Anonymous (1)

Art & Kobbie Alamo

Ann E. Beman

Carmen Bernier Grand

Janet Buttenwieser

Sylvia Chambers

Claire Gebben

Marie Hartung

James

Debbie Lang

Rev. Kyle Lovett

Marian Robinson and
Sue Vahrenkamp

Synergistic Creations

Diane Van der Linde

Neal and Pam Washburn

_____

Allie & Joz

Anonymous (4)

Sharon Andrews

Ian T.Bawn

Bonny Becker

Lois Brandt

Blaine Carpenter

Chris Conkling

Robert Cserni

Searah Deysach

Jen Fineran

Laurie Fox

Cathy Franchett

Iris Graville

Bill Gould

Stephanie Barbe Hammer

Karen Hirsch

Grier Jewell

Mary Kabrich

Alexis Klein

Tom Knoblauch

Sandi Kurtz

Chuck Lennox

Stephanie Lile

Lizzy

Tammy Luthy

Lena Mentyka

Mo

Janet Neuhauser

Trudi and Joe Picciano

Joe Ponepinto

Junet J. Rabin

Elizabeth Ralston

Andrew and Caroline Rozendal

Julie Shapiro and Shelly F. Cohen

Matthew Sorenson

Barb Stafki

Patrick Swett

Laurie Ann Thompson

Saralyn L. Tossetti

Samantha Claire Updegrave

Kirk Wheeler

CPSIA information can be obtained at www.ICGtesting.com
Printed in the USA
LVIW01n2151070715
445371LV00008B/23